Blut and Boden
A Fairy Tale for Children of European Descent

ASH DONALDSON

www.preservationoffire.com

Books by Ash Donaldson:

Mythology Series

Blut and Boden: A Fairy Tale for Children of European Descent

A Race for the North: Another Fairy Tale for Children of European Descent

Brother War: A Modern Myth for Those of European Descent

Novel

From Her Eyes a Doctrine

Copyright © 2019 Ash Donaldson

All rights reserved.

ISBN-13: 978-1725740419

DEDICATION

For my children

CONTENTS

1 The Ancient Ones   1
2 The Five Kingdoms   9
3 Blut and Boden   17
4 The Winter King   27
5 The Return   35
6 A Young Boy   45
7 Night of Fire   57
   Historical Note   70
   Illustration Credits   71

FOREWORD

This is a book for the young, but one that older readers may also enjoy. Many parents and grandparents feel that we do not belong to this time and place, and we fear that our children feel it, too. To have a homeland, a place where you belong, only to lose it might be worse than never having a home in the first place. But we should always have hope, as long as we remember how special our people are. For we also carry our home with us, in our blood. And wherever we go, our blood mixes with the soil as we labor and fight for it.

In one of the languages of our race, German, the word for blood is *Blut*, pronounced to rhyme with "flute." And the word for soil is *Boden*, with a long "o" sound. Long ago, perhaps, there were two magical creatures, Elves they were, named Blut and Boden. I hope you will enjoy their story and find inspiration in it.

ASH DONALDSON

CHAPTER 1
THE ANCIENT ONES

Long ago, creatures of might and power roamed the earth: Giants, Elves, Dwarves, and the sprites and fairies that live in every glade and glen. You might not think it, but they are with us still, as you will see. This is their story, and yours, as well.

The oldest of all beings are the Giants. At least that is what they say, and no one is old enough to contradict them. Perhaps you think that they must be big, and they certainly can be if they want. But they can be any size they choose, even the size of a man. Giants prefer to be big, though, because they are vain and want to show their power. And powerful they certainly are, for they are nothing more nor less than the forces of nature let loose.

In fact, the old name for Giants had nothing to do with size. They were called simply *the Devourers*. That is because if they are not checked, they will take everything, destroying and devouring. Giants never give a thought to anything but what they want.

Because they are the wild forces of nature, some of the Giants lies within you, for you, too, are a part of nature. If you gave in to every desire and urge, you would be like a Giant, although a rather weak one at that. But you can choose to tame these forces inside yourself and make them serve higher purposes. For you have a higher nature and a higher calling. To follow it is not easy. But struggle is what life is all about.

The old stories tell us of many kinds of Giants, above all those of fire and frost, sea and storm. Fire Giants love to feed and devour all that burns, until their cry becomes a loud roar. Yet even in the smallest fire you can hear their hungry whisper. Many times you may have watched a fire and found it hard to look away, for fire is a kindred spirit. Like you, it is restless and always wants more.

Frost Giants possess an altogether different nature. They want to fill the land with bone-chilling cold. Unable to escape the coldness of their nature, they do not want anyone else to, either. You could be like that if you chose. Just as too much of the cold kills animals and plants, so can coldness of the heart kill warmth and love among our family and friends.

We also find stories of Storm Giants, who fill the sky with dark clouds, raging in thunder and lightning and wind. There are times when it is all right to be angry. But perhaps you have gotten so hateful that you enjoy it, and in you is room for nothing but that rage. If so, then you know a bit of what this Storm Giant nature feels like.

Sea Giants command great power, enough to change the face of the earth. Like fire, however, they can mislead, appearing calm one minute and churning into dangerous waves the next. Even the most skilled sailors fear the power of the sea, and it has dragged many down into its depths. Perhaps there have been times when you are pouting, yet when someone asks you what's wrong, you say, "Nothing," even though dark thoughts trouble you. Then you have some idea of the gloomy mystery of Sea Giants.

Keep in mind that Giants are no more evil than nature is evil. Some of the most beautiful things in nature are giantish. The winds that can capsize a ship at sea are also what moves the sailboat along. The storm that strikes down trees also brings rain, which carries life to the soil. Fire, too, can give life, so long as it is kept within limits.

You will never be able to see a Giant in any form other than these, unless they want you to. And if I were you, I would not hope for such a moment, for according to the old stories, it can be terrifying to behold a Giant face to face.

While not as old as the Giants, Elves are an ancient race. They shape nature into great works of beauty, which we enjoy in all seasons. If you have ever looked closely at a flower and marveled at how each one seems to be crafted by hand, then you have admired the work of Elves. With the help of fairies and other spirits of the land, they make the earth fruitful.

If you have ever been in a forest and heard a rustle, but there was no bird or animal nearby, you might just have come close to an Elf. We are similar to Elves in appearance and size, and you might not even realize it if you met one, especially if they did not want you to know. But they are too quick to be seen if they do not wish to be.

The Elves take the things of nature and make them even more beautiful. That is not so different from you, when you draw a picture with great care or create a beautiful melody, taking the time to make it just right. In that wonderful place where work and play blend together, there lies your Elvish nature.

According to our lore, Elves can live forever, but death can still come in two ways. They can be killed, but that does not happen easily. Elves are great warriors and have had ages to train. Many fought against the Giants in wars only they remember. I will soon tell you of one.

They can also die if they no longer wish to live. Then it is said that they die of a broken heart. To live so long is not easy, especially if you see your home destroyed and the ones you love killed. Elves have a deep sadness within, surpassing that of any other creature. Yet they also know great joy, and many stories tell of how they dance among the trees and green grass in their secret haunts.

I must also tell you of a third race, the Dwarves, for they figure in this story, as well. Some refer to Dwarves as the "Dark Elves." Long ago, they say, some of the Elves wanted a greater challenge. They would work not on flowers or trees but on the hardest things in nature: the rocks and metals, the very bones of the earth. And so these Elves tunneled deep underground to search for gold and silver and copper. One day, their tunnels reached so deep that these Elves did not come back to the surface. Instead, they built their homes deep beneath the roots of mountains, carving their dwellings out of rock.

The Dwarves work with hammer and fire to craft objects more dazzling than any you have seen. The beauty of many an Elf-lady has been rendered more wondrous still by a Dwarf-made necklace or brooch, bracelet or earrings. Few are the human women fortunate enough to have worn such an ornament.

But Dwarves also forge weapons legendary for their strength and might: axes and spears, swords and shields. Only a few Dwarf-made swords ever came into human hands, but each one had a name

and cut a swath through history. Most of these weapons, however, have never seen the light of day. They lie in huge caverns, awaiting some future war of which the Dwarves know but never speak. One day those store-houses will be opened, and astonishing weapons of great beauty and power will glitter in the sun. But that will happen only when things are at their worst, so it is best not to hope for that day.

Dwarves are known to be the most patient of creatures. A Dwarf can work several human lifetimes on just one sword, or just one necklace, if he is determined to make it perfect. They are tough creatures who do not mind hardship. Perhaps you have been at a task, and part of you thinks that it is too difficult, that you should quit, but you stick with it anyway. That is because of Dwarf-might within you. That perseverance helps many a man or woman of our race to do what needs to be done. But persistence can also become stubbornness, and according to the proverb, it is easier to move a mountain than to get a Dwarf to change his mind.

We think of Dwarves as short, even though they can be our size if they so choose. That is because they prefer to be close to the earth they love.

Now, dear reader, you are ready to hear my tale.

CHAPTER 2
THE FIVE KINGDOMS

  Long ago, in the land we call North America, five elven kingdoms once stood, and their glory endured for countless ages. If you have ever had a dream so wonderful that you wanted to fall right back asleep and return to that other world, you might have been given a glimpse of some corner of those Elf-realms of splendor.

  For eons, the Giant clans warred upon one other, and so it was easier to keep them at bay. Giants of land and sea re-shaped the world itself in their strife. But there came a time when the Frost Giants united under a fearsome leader named Grim Jack. Even to this day, when the cold winter wind bites at our cheeks and frosts the windows, we joke that it is "Jack Frost." But if you could see him in all his terrible glory, you would know why even the other Giants dreaded him. It was their fear that united them.

  Even the Giants of Storm and Fire and Sea kept away as the Frost Giants advanced in a vast army from the cold North. Everywhere they marched came a winter that did not end, and the plants and animals perished. Onward the Giants pressed to the South, until they reached the green forests and flower-fields of the five elven kingdoms.

  The five Elf-kings, proud as Elves are of their independence, each took thought only for his own kingdom. Never did all five

together take the field against Grim Jack. Battles untold raged across the centuries, and much Elf-blood was shed, for the Frost Giants hated the Elves, and the Elves were fighting for all they held dear.

One by one the five kings fell at the hands of the Frost Giants, who left their kingdoms in ruins. The surviving Elves left all they had loved and boarded ships for another land. I will tell you of it soon enough, but first you must learn what happened during this time, which the Elves call the Scouring. This is because the surface of the land was scraped and flattened by the great glaciers that moved with the Frost Giants.

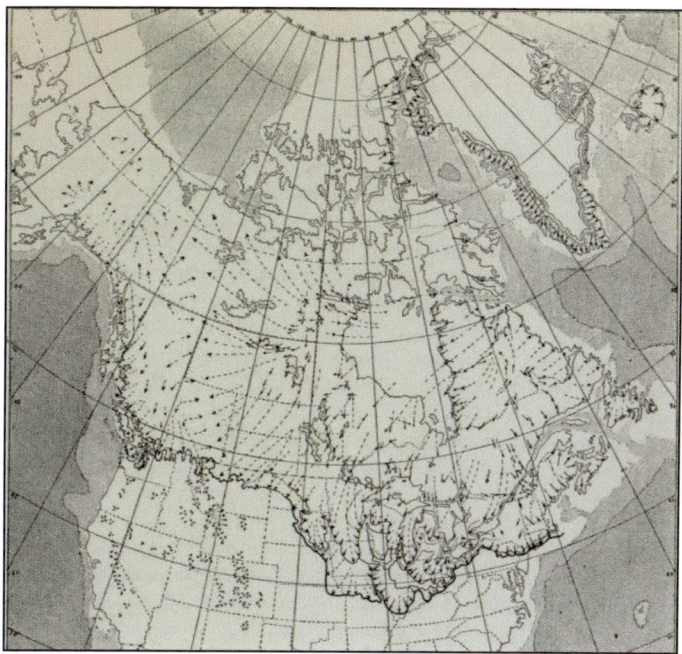

It was at the hour of the Frost Giants' victory over the last Elf-king that something unexpected happened. There was a Giant-maiden named Gerda, fair of face and fair in character, too. For she was one of those Giants who are wild but do not love destruction, appearing to us as a flowing river, or the tides, or a gentle snow flurry. Only a little step, perhaps, separates them from having an elvish nature. Gerda took that step when she saw how the Elves lived, and how they died. She looked upon the beauty of their realms, watched them crushed under glaciers, and lamented when the last Elves had left.

Now Grim Jack had a son named Hail, and he had fallen in love with Gerda. Hail couldn't see the elvish beauty the way she did, for he was very much like his father, except that he loved Gerda. That made things difficult. For when Grim Jack ordered the Frost Giants to continue south until all life was gone from the land, Gerda defied his command. Even though all the Frost Giants cowered before Grim Jack, she stood in his way and said they had done enough.

Grim Jack was a Giant through and through, so to him there was no such thing as "enough." Outraged that Gerda would dare to oppose him, he made to strike her down and would have, but Hail jumped in front of his father. In truth, he was terrified, but he would do anything to protect Gerda. Grim Jack's eyes blazed in anger as he looked upon his son, and in one mighty blow he struck him down. Hail's enormous body hit the earth with a great crash, and Gerda screamed in anguish at the death of her beloved.

Even for the Giants, to kill a son was a foul deed. By that act, Grim Jack had lost his standing with the Frost Giants, and none would follow him again. As Gerda held Hail's body, the Giants set to quarreling. The army broke up, the Giants dispersed, and the glaciers slowly withdrew.

Two extraordinary things happened then. First, when Gerda lay down beside her beloved Hail, the warmth of her love melted the ice of her Frost Giant nature, and it flowed as tears. So still they lay through the long ages, Gerda and Hail, that their Giant bodies became as rock. In time, trees grew upon them, and animals came to live there. And still Gerda sat watching Hail, only her tears had become a river, a river that still flows. For you should know that Hail lies on the east side, and Gerda lies on the west, and between them her tears form the Mississippi, a river of sadness and enduring love.

As for Grim Jack, it is said that when the cold winter wind blows from the North, you can hear him mourning for his son, yet still raging against him.

The second remarkable thing was this: as the glaciers retreated from the kingdoms they had leveled, in the center of each realm a a huge lake formed from the melting ice. We call them the Great Lakes, but buried somewhere below lies the heart of each elven kingdom. There beneath the waters sit long-dead monarchs, placed once more on their thrones by devoted retainers, looking with lifeless eyes upon halls in which their subjects once vied for glory.

Although the remaining Elves left that land, the smaller creatures, the fairies and sprites, still tended to nature as best they could. And from the Rocky Mountains far to the West came the Dwarves. They had heard that the Elf-kingdoms were no more, and here and there in the woods they found the ruins of elven homes. The Dwarves began to tunnel underneath the Five Kingdoms, for the land near the lakes was rich in iron and copper, silver and gold. There, far beneath where Elves had once danced and feasted and loved, the Dwarves built their dark halls and lit their forges.

As the glaciers retreated, another group arrived in that land: humans. We are not descended from these people, however, for they came from Asia, a land far across the western ocean. They were men of darker skin, not black but more like the copper that lies in the earth. We call them Indians, and they lived in a land without horses or cattle, and they knew neither the wheel nor the ship. Swords, too, they lacked, although they fought one another with great savagery. They had no inkling of the great war that had been fought here long before they came.

As for the Elves who survived the Scouring, they embarked on ships and sailed in the opposite direction, to where the sun rises. With them came a young Elf-prince named Boden, the only prince left alive, in fact. His father's kingdom, further south and west, had been the last to fall. When Boden's father saw at last that the end had come, he put his wife, son, and daughter in a boat, and the four of them sought to escape. Grim Jack, however, arrived with all the force and speed of a blizzard.

To give his family time to get away, Boden's father challenged Grim Jack to a fight he knew he would lose. The queen could not abandon her husband so easily, and so she was there when the Frost Giant ran him through with a spear. Her heart broke at the sight, and she ran to him, tending to her dying husband as Grim Jack gloated.

Young Boden tried to row himself and his young sister away, for while Grim Jack might scoff at slaying a woman, he would allow no Elf-prince to live. Amid the storm-tossed waves, however, the boat

capsized, and his sister disappeared into the water's icy grip. Boden searched for her in the surge, but other Elves pulled the boy onto a ship and sailed away before Grim Jack could stop them. Thus Boden left the kingdom that would have been his birthright.

This remnant of the Elves landed in a place we call Europe, a land that reminded them of home, with deep forests and rushing rivers. Here they found distant relatives, Elf-kin who had settled here when the world was young.

    But they also found another war, for the Frost Giants had invaded this land, as well, seeking to destroy the order and beauty that the Elves of Europe had made. Boden's guardians saw to it that he, the last Elf-prince of the West, grew up far from the ravages of that war. But destiny would call him to it, just as it would call forth a new, unexpected race. That is the next part of my tale.

CHAPTER 3
BLUT AND BODEN

Young Boden grew up in the mountains of Carpathia, and he soon proved to be clever, bold, and skilled in magic. While all Elves possess some skill in magic, Boden was truly a lord of nature. If he so chose, wherever he stepped, there a new tree would grow behind him. He could make each tree rise up full grown all at once, so that, running through a barren field, he could transform it into a forest in the blink of an eye.

But that was not all. If Boden raised his palms to the sky, he could make a newly formed bird appear above each one – any sort of bird he wished, from a tiny wren to a mighty eagle. And if he held his palms facing down, to the earth, beneath each one would emerge a wild animal – any sort of animal he wished, from a wee field mouse to a great stag. Thus Boden could make a place flourish with plants and animals very quickly.

Boden learned to fight, as well, for even far from the front lines, he would come upon Frost Giants. Already in his youth, he gained fame for his manly daring, and the sword he wielded became known as the Giants' Bane. You must understand that Elves are not slight, frail beings who never harm anything. Beset by many enemies, they have fought more wars through the ages of the Earth than any creature, and no Giant has as much wrath as an Elf who has been

angered.

    Wild and free Boden lived, but he could not escape the terrible conflict known as the Winter War, which had been raging long before his arrival. Many kingdoms succumbed, as had those in the West. But the Elves of Europe had help from an unlikely place.

    Some mortal men had joined the Elves in their struggle against the Giants, for their homes also lay here. Only a few did so, for most men had no desire to face the cold and the wrath of Frost Giants, choosing to remain instead in the sunnier lands to the South. The few who dwelled in Europe were a hardy breed. Little sunlight shone here, and the winters were so long as to seem endless. Those who had darker skin did not take in as much light as their bodies needed, and they grew weak and sick. The ones who survived had the whitest skin.

    Over many hundreds of generations in that cruel war, other changes came about. The survivors had narrower noses, to warm up the cold air before it came into their lungs. While those in the South chased quickly after the animals of the plain, the men of the North

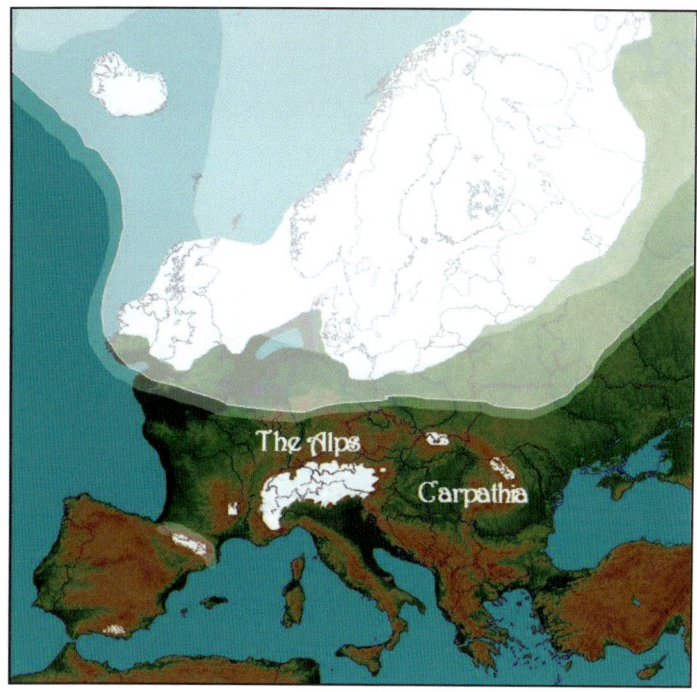

were gone for weeks, hunting great beasts that once roamed those frozen wastes. They needed strength more than speed, and the ability to endure.

Those in the farthest North, on the front lines of the war, lived where the sun barely rises in winter, and on a few days there is no sun at all. They had blue or green eyes to take in more light, and many of them had hair that was red or blond.

And so the men of this war not only fought alongside the Elves; they and their women came to look more like the Elves than all the races of man, with a stout, Dwarf-like toughness. This happened over many thousands of years, for the Winter War was longer and more terrible than any war before or since.

Thus was this new race shaped in outward form. But inside, as well, these men and women were being forged like a sword on a Dwarf's anvil, and their children grew up tough. Unlike the races in sunnier lands, who could survive year-round with or without dwellings, those of northern Europe had to build houses that could withstand the long, harsh winter. Those who did not build well died from the cold. To find food in the frigid winter is not easy, so only the cleverest survived. They went on long hunts across frozen landscapes that one could scarcely navigate. To survive, they had to reason, remember, and plan.

So difficult was it to hunt animals in the cold North, that many families might be kept from starvation by only one hunter's find. Thus, the tribe survived through its members showing kindness, always thinking the best of one another. To bring down the huge mastodons that once lived in Europe, they had to work together, decide quickly, and take risks that might end someone's life. Being willing to sacrifice oneself for the common good became the highest virtue among them.

To survive meant planning well, saving enough food and wood, and preparing for the winter while it was still warm outside – to see things that are not here but one day will be. They had to rise in the night to keep the winter-fires burning, fighting off sleep and comfort, or else death would come there in the frozen North. With patience and forethought, they put off what they wanted until what they had to do was done.

Everyone pitched in, from the youngest to the oldest, and they valued hard work as much as any Dwarf. The harshness of life made every life precious, even the smallest child, for only if their family was strong did they survive. They held their women in higher regard than any men on earth, and to be true to each other was not only a virtue, but a necessity for survival.

Deep in their soul, too, they became more elvish, for the Elves had a sadness inside that has been with our race ever since. From them we get our sense of lost glory, of a golden age long gone. We feel it in our bones, that things are not as they should be, that the world is in decline, and that it will get worse – until the sleeper awakens.

Thus, they slowly became like both Elves and Dwarves, this new race. The Elves dubbed them the sons of Arius, or Aryans, those descended from the Noble One.

Yet always, like any man, this race had the giantish impulses waiting to be fed. Much beauty can be shaped from Giant-nature, as both Elves and Dwarves know. But for that, one needs to be a master of one's drives and not a slave to them. Otherwise, you can create no true beauty.

In that land of Europe, in the little corner of Carpathia, the Elf-prince from across the sea heard tidings of a great massing of Frost Giants, and that his race was in peril. For while the Giants had suffered many losses, now they had slain the last of the Elf-kings. From all sides their armies marched, seeking to wipe out their age-old enemies at last, and they were led by one known as the Winter King. A Giant every bit as fearsome as Grim Jack, he had been butchering the sons of Arius for ages, and many an Elf, too, had fallen under his great club.

The last of the Elf-kings to fall in the defense of his people had a daughter named Blut. She now gathered the remaining Elves into the mountains of the Alps to make a final stand. The sons of Arius, who had fought alongside Blut's kindred for many thousands of years, did not abandon the Elves in their hour of greatest need. By tribes they

...nd Blut welcomed them.

...troubled court of that Elf-princess came Boden one day, ...a gallant figure even among those hardy knights. Many an ...n wished for his love, but he saw that none were as fair, none as enchanting, as Blut.

Oh, the beauty of Blut! How can I describe it? Her hair had the unique quality of changing color throughout the day. At dawn, its red matched the horizon, then as day came, it slowly blended into a blond that equaled the shining sun. At sunset, her hair reddened once more, then darkened from chestnut brown at twilight to raven black at midnight. With the coming of dawn, it lightened again.

But that was not all — the color of her eyes altered with the seasons. In summer, their green was like the trees that sigh softly in the northern forests. As the leaves began to change color in autumn, her eyes became hazel with gold flecks, then amber passing into light brown. But in winter, her eyes became as gray as the sky that could be seen between the bare tree branches. Then, with the coming of spring, her eyes deepened into blue like the rains that wash away the snow and bring life, whereupon they became green once more. So beautiful was Blut, men said it was not her eyes that matched the seasons, but the seasons of earth that tried to copy her eyes.

Depending on the time of day and season, Blut's eyes and hair had truly endless combinations of color. For because the hues changed gradually rather than all at once, you never saw her in quite the same way. But always she had the lovely white skin that set off each color perfectly.

This radiant mix of colors for hair and eyes we find in the race of Arius. No other race of man possesses it, so that some call it Blut's Gift. In truth, this snow-forged race received many such gifts from her. They say that every painting, every sculpture of a woman is but men's feeble attempt to recreate the beauty of Blut, which they find reflected in the woman they adore. In every daring deed a man does, every effort he puts his whole heart into, he is driven by the inspiration Blut's beauty stirs in him, embodied in his true love. Thus

does this race-memory course down through the ages. How else to explain why the sons of Arius have been the greatest inventors and creators?

Most striking of all was the necklace Blut wore. Dwarf-made but touched with Elf-craft as well, it was a heart suspended on a necklace, crimson in color but like nothing else on earth. For the more you looked at it, the more there appeared to be something going on inside of it. If a man looked closely into its depths, he became speechless so long as he beheld it, and afterwards, he could not remember what he had seen.

A mystery lies within the Radiant Heart, as it was called, and I cannot tell you what it is, for I do not know. They say it was forged at the dawning of the world, and that the Giants would most like to have it. If the Devourers ever did come to possess it, the creative spark would leave the sons of Arius and Elf-kind alike.

They say, too, that babies know the secret when they are in the womb. When they come into this world, they cry night and day because they cannot share it. And when they first smile, it is because their mother's face reminds them of Blut. They have no way to tell it, however, and as they grow, their memories fade, until at last, it appears only in dreams.

One can easily see how this mistress of the Elves would captivate Boden, and how this dashing prince might win Blut's heart where none before had. Their romance is the stuff of legend, and many a poet and writer has tried to describe it. For every love story is a distant memory of this one, which echoes through the ages like a note played on a harp, lingering in the air long after the hand has plucked the string.

As must be the case for every man, however, it is not enough to love a woman; he must be willing to fight for her. How Boden did so is the next part of my tale.

CHAPTER 4
THE WINTER KING

I was there, I tell you, at the final battle, when Boden fought. It may only have been in dreams, but dreams can show a deeper truth than we know with the waking mind. There, at the foot of the Alps, a vast number of Giants thronged, and in front stood the Winter King himself, with his death-dealing club.

Facing him across the field were Elf-knights firm of purpose, but few in number now, the mere shadow of former glory. On either side, arrayed in battle lines, came warriors from the young race of Arius. Tough men they were, true sons of their fathers, yet when the Winter King stepped forth, many a man, though wrapped in warm furs, set to shivering when he beheld that beast.

In a voice that shook the ground, the Winter King bellowed: "Puny race of men, surely you must know that with this club I have shed the blood of your fathers and grandfathers, on back through the centuries. But come, step forward, and mingle your blood with theirs! My club longs to scatter your bones across these fields for the crows to feast upon!" At this the Frost Giants howled, and the sound came across the field as an ice-cold winter wind.

Then that king of Giants looked upon the Elves in their gleaming armor. "Wretched Elves!" his voice boomed. "All the more wretched for lacking a king! Is this all that remains of those great armies I once faced? But if you insist, I will send you to your doom as I have been doing for a long span, long even for an Elf! For I was there when the world was created out of fire and ice. And in ice if not fire all that you do will be undone!"

Then the ranks of Elf-knights parted, and there before them appeared Blut in all her glory, the Radiant Heart upon her breast. The host of Giants gave out a groan because they wanted her — it was in fact for her as prize that they fought. For if she could be captured, there would be no more striving, no more creating. Elf, Dwarf, and man alike would wallow in sloth and weakness, turning inward while the Giants rended the universe from top to bottom. They wanted her and yet they hated her, hated her for her beauty and her power to inspire. There she stood, her gaze queenly, her radiance beyond words.

The ranks parted once more, and Boden strode forth, his armor sparkling in the light reflected from glaciers. Sheathed at his side was the Giants' Bane. Never before had these Giants looked upon Boden; they had only heard tales of the wild forest-elf in Carpathia. Now they watched, waiting to see what would happen.

And while they stand there in expectation, let me tell you what did not happen. There might be some who would wish that Blut as well as Boden would charge the Giants' battle-line. They might imagine that Blut, the matchless Elf-maid, pulled out a bow and shot arrows into the enemy. Or that maybe she hefted a sword and wielded it in battle. But such people are confused. That is not surprising, for we live in a confusing age.

Know that a woman, be she Elf or human, receives the highest honor for what she *is*, not for what she *does*. It is what she *is*, her honor, her beauty, her grace, and her lightness of heart that has the power to command men more surely than any king's scepter. Whereas a man attains his highest honor not for what he *is*, but for what he *does*. A man's greatest joy comes from striving, shedding sweat and blood to bestow upon his lady a worthy gift, and her happiness lies in receiving his attentions. Great confusion arises because people forget this truth, and so we have women today who try to be like men, and men who try to be like women, and little joy to show for it.

No one could forget this truth who watched that scene where the glaciers met the mountains. Turning from that dreadful army of Giants, Boden, Elf-prince and sole heir to the Five Kingdoms, stepped before Blut and knelt before her. "What is your wish, my lady?" he asked.

Blut looked down at him, and upon her breast lay the Radiant Heart, swirling fiercely inside. She thought of her father and her brothers, cut down as they defended their people. Her eyes flashed through all the colors of the seasons before returning to gray, for in this place it was always winter. "I wish for slaughter, and an end to this war."

She wished for slaughter! How the ears of any true man would thrill to hear such a thing from his lady, to send him to the fight no matter how perilous! For a man longs to defend his true love, and doing so he would smile though the heavens fall around him. So, now, did Boden smile. Then he kissed the hand of his beloved before rising to his full stature.

Turning back to the enemy, Boden stepped in front of his army. The Winter King, sizing him up, roared, "Might this be the Elf-prince I have heard of, who fled when my brother Grim Jack smashed the Five Kingdoms? Come here, then, and meet your father's doom!" Then he laughed, and the rest of the Frost Giants with him.

Boden said nothing, only raised his hands out before him, palms down. With a flash of light, a stag appeared on his right side, and a wolf on his left. They pawed the ground, ready to advance, but the wolf did not attack the stag, and the stag did not fear the wolf. This curious fact troubled the Giants even more than the animals' sudden appearance, for it meant dominion over nature – and Giants are, after all, forces of nature.

The Elf-prince brought his hands closer together, and flash – in front of him appeared a grizzly bear, the kind he had known once in his father's kingdom. With a graceful jump Boden leapt on its back, and it allowed him to mount, carrying him like a war horse. This steed, however, sported not hooves but massive paws with deadly talons.

Riding the huge bear, with the stag and the wolf beside him, Boden began to move forward, slowly at first, but gaining speed. The bear began to charge, and up went Boden's hands again – flash – and there was another stag and another wolf, born running, ready to join their companions. Flash! A third pair, and then another, and again, and again, and soon they formed a great wedge coming toward the enemy. In front rode Boden atop the bear, with the first stag and wolf close by, and in ranks sweeping back on either side, hundreds of wolves and stags, antlers tossing, wolf-teeth bared.

As they raced on, the Elf-prince raised his palms to the sky, and flash – there appeared an eagle on his right and a hawk on his left, soaring high above him. As Boden kept his hands raised, his legs hugging the bear beneath him, hawks and eagles began to fill the sky, forming a wedge above like the one below.

Facing this onrushing army so unlike any they had met, the Frost Giants nervously stamped their feet. They now knew a fear that they had never felt before. As they watched, Boden, close now to their own ranks and nearing fast, unsheathed the Giants' Bane and raised it high. And it was as if all the light that shimmers off snow and ice glanced off that blade and shot back, blinding those Frost Giants for a moment. When vision returned to them, it brought the sight of Boden, noblest of Elf-knights and lord of nature, aiming that fearsome sword right at the Winter King as he rode straight on.

As the Elf-prince came within range, the mighty Frost Giant swung his huge club sideways to knock him across the field, but Boden's bear-mount took a great leap and bounded over it. As the bear came down upon the Giant, tearing at him savagely, his rider thrust that dreaded blade right into the Winter King's chest. With a terrible scream the fearsome Giant collapsed, never to rise again.

As he lay dying on the snowy ground, the last thing the Frost Giant heard was the triumphant shout of Elf-kind and the sons of Arius. Eagerly they started across the field to strike at their ancient foes. While they rushed across, wolves and stags continued to drive deep into the enemy ranks, leaving many a hole in the Giant host, as birds of prey swooped down. Yet when men and Elves reached that battle, they found it no easy fight. Those ancient powers of nature fought with might and main. Vast numbers of men paid with their lives that day, as did the Elves. In the end, however, the Frost Giants who stood their ground fell dead upon it, while those who fled became like the winter wind, swept away to the North.

I saw it, I tell you, that day when Boden avenged the loss of his land by winning a new one. After slogging back across the field of battle, he stood before Blut and offered her the mighty club of the Winter King as prize. The dead had been collected, and all that remained were the bodies of Frost Giants in heaps where they fell. Boden went down on one knee before her, and the moment his knee hit the ground a great rumble sounded far out on the battlefield. She gave him her hand, and he stood up. Both peered into the distance with their keen Elf eyes.

The Frost Giants' bodies had turned to ice, their native form, and the sound the victors heard was that ice cracking under the newfound strength of the sun. For a race so ancient, it melted all too quickly. In a matter of minutes, before the victors lay an enormous lake. Looking upon that sea, Blut bade him throw the Giant's evil club in it, and when Boden did so, it sank into the deep. Ever since, that water has borne his name.

CHAPTER 5
THE RETURN

Thus did the Elves of Europe, joined now by the survivors from the Five Kingdoms, beat back the Frost Giants with the help of this young race, the sons of Arius. Then began the days of freedom, and the renewing of the land. Once the Winter War ended, and the glaciers began to retreat, men settled the new lands to the North that the Elves had crafted into the most beautiful place on earth. Here stark mountains reached for the sky, and rolling hills of green ran to meet the sea, whose dark waves crashed on shore, leaving beautiful amber on the beach.

The Elves had lived there long before the Winter War, but they were too few now to hold claim to all of this. They recognized, also, that this race of men had earned some right to this land. Over the course of hundreds of men's lifetimes, the Elves had come to respect this people, who had endured so much as they were shaped into this Elf-like, Dwarf-like race.

Some of the Elves chose to leave, for there are other worlds besides this one, although few as lovely. But they are a sentimental people, and many could not bear to part with a land upon which their very memories were etched. They retreated instead to places of quiet refuge in a continent that was gradually traversed by the roads of men.

The Elves still met with the sons of Arius on great occasions, and then the Elf-warriors would remind them of how bravely their human ancestors had fought. To the Elves, you see, these events were as yesterday, even though many generations of men had come and gone. Gradually, however, the festive occasions became fewer, the span of time too long, and the Elves slowly withdrew from men's company. They passed into legend.

The Dwarves, by nature even more private, had been so impressed with the qualities of this new race of men that even they emerged from their underground realms to speak with them. Like the Dwarves, the sons of Arius craved order and worked hard for it. And so the Dwarves bestowed gifts. One was the forging of bronze, made from copper and tin, which helped man make better tools and sharper weapons. Another was the wheel, which enabled man to make wagons, so that beasts of burden could carry his things for him. The Dwarves' final gift, the smelting of iron, began a new age, for iron is so useful that it saves man much labor. Then, with the gifts received and thanks given, the Dwarves, too, retreated into legend.

The Elves had not left the sons of Arius giftless, either, for they showed them how to tame the horse. So strongly did these men bond with the horse, that even now we feel the race-memory draw us to this animal: we sense its nobility, and we respect its power. It stirs our blood to see a horse gallop, and we know not the reason. The sons of Arius took the Elf-gift of horse-taming and the Dwarf-gift of the wheeled cart and from them made the horse and chariot. With this, they swept over their enemies and kept themselves free.

As for the Frost Giants, although they had suffered a great defeat, they were still a force to be reckoned with, and remain so even now. For every year they begin their march, bringing on the winter, until they are beaten back by those Elves who still guard the land. Whenever you feel the winter chill right down to your bones, you taste a bit of the Frost Giants' wrath, although their power is much diminished these days from what our ancestors faced.

And so generation followed generation, and thousands of years passed. To men, the years were long, for even one century is as much as a mortal man can hope to live. But to the Elves, who have lived here since the spring-time of the earth, the years seemed to pass like days. Everything changed too quickly for those who remembered the Winter War, and the long summer before.

The sons of Arius grew in number, and their towns soon dotted the land. Through their cleverness, they made life easier for themselves, but a soft life can produce soft men. Yet valor could still be found among them, as when three hundred men fought in a narrow pass against three million invaders from Asia, dying so that their wives and children might live free.

Courage was also in those who took to the sea. Into the

unknown they sailed, risking the wrath of Sea Giants and Storm Giants. But they persisted, and by force of an iron will, they overcame the odds. With great daring they crossed the ocean toward the sunset, reaching at last the land where the Five Kingdoms once stood. A race unlike themselves they found there, not Elves but men. To this land the sons of Arius brought the gifts that Elves and Dwarves had given them: the wheel and the forge, the plow and the horse, weapons and tools of iron. These gifts had already spread far beyond their homeland, but not yet across the ocean.

This western land stirred their blood, for it seemed like their own homeland as their ancestors must have known it, wild and lush. This vast continent was not free for the taking, however, since the copper-skinned men who lived there fought for it. These Indians were a tough race of warriors, and they had been warring upon each other since they first arrived, long after the Elf-realms sank under the water.

The sons of Arius did not steal the land, as some men say. They won it by shedding their own blood, and by the sweat of working the land and making it yield up its riches. For though the sons of Arius can appreciate the beauty of the earth because of the Elf-nature that is in them, like the Dwarves they also long to make something with it, as a testament to their skill and an inheritance for their children. For those on the frontier, life proved every bit as harsh as what their ancestors had faced long ago, during the forging of their race. With blood and sweat they bought the land and paid in full.

They did not come alone. For in the hearts of Boden's people stirred a longing to return to their ancient land. The western Elves knew there would be no bringing back the vanished glory of the Five Kingdoms, for they were but a small remnant of those who had fought Grim Jack, only to face the Winter King across the field of Boden. Yet, while the ruined center of each kingdom was buried under water, around those seas were the same forested lands they had known, where they had lived and loved for ages.

And so now they returned, not in great numbers on ships of their own, as when they had fled Grim Jack, but in ones and twos, as the spirit moved them. They boarded the ships of the sons of Arius disguised as mortal men. That was easy to do, for most people think of themselves as too clever to believe in Elves. They give credence only to what they themselves are capable of; anything more, they doubt. If they cannot see it with their own eyes, they scoff and call it legend.

Still, there were moments when the disguise nearly failed:

"Look at that man, *señor*, the one who wears his armor so well. He is a *conquistador*, I do not doubt it. But there is something odd about him. I was walking on deck last night and saw him staring out to sea, and I tell you his sword *glowed* in the night – it glowed! Never have I seen such a sword. With that, he could slay many a man. You would do well not to bother him."

"Have you seen that young woman, Jacques? I have never seen a young lady so lovely! I talked with her last night, and her voice was like the soft tinkling of chimes, so pretty. You don't believe me? Well, don't try your luck with her, for she told me that her husband had passed on to the next world, but she wasn't about to replace him in this. '*Madame*,' says I, 'whatever happened to him?' 'He died in a great battle over *there*,' she said, and pointed west. Now I ask you, Jacques, has any war been fought in New France for twenty years? Then how can she be a widow? She's a strange one, she is."

"Sir Oliver, I write to report that this colony is thriving, but I cannot take the credit. We have a young couple here who have started a farm with the most extraordinary success. Everything they set their mind to flourishes: no seed is wasted, the fields never fail, and the animals are in perfect health. I can't explain it. Without these two, many of us would have perished. Sadly, they have declared their intention to head further west. I've warned them, of course, that they are certain to be killed by the Indians, but at this, they only smiled. Alas, what is to become of them?"

And so the western Elves returned to the places where they had known so much joy and sadness, in the lands around the Great Lakes. There they came upon the Dwarves' tunnels under the earth, for while they are hidden from the eye of man, the eyes of an Elf can find them easily enough. They did not begrudge the Dwarves the riches underground. Besides, the sons of Arius would soon be here.

The Elves would live in the shadows, as they had across the sea in Europe.

When the sons of Arius arrived in the northern woods, the Elves bore them no ill will. They befriended those who had dared such a dangerous journey, and it was almost like in those days, long ago, when the races dwelt in friendship. For though the Elves did not reveal who they were, they shared their knowledge of this land with the first pioneers. They were among the first rivermen, who bravely voyaged in canoes down the rapids and into strange forests. They taught men to roll logs down the river, walking gracefully atop the floating beams, never missing a step.

The prosperous Dwarves, too, were content to share their knowledge. For here came men who, like themselves, were intent on finding the metal riches within the earth. With the wealth from the mines, the sons of Arius were building ships, laying down railroad tracks, and conquering a continent:

> "See that stout, bearded fellow over there? I tell you, he is a godsend. Never does he tell us to dig without it becoming a mother-lode. And I have never seen an abler man with axe or hammer. Only it's odd, when I asked him where a man with his accent might be from, he told me he was Finnish, but the Finns insisted he was German. Yet the men from Cornwall claim him as one of their own."

Long after these mysterious companions left, miners would leave out food for these little men who would still knock on the tunnel walls to warn them of a cave-in, giving them time to escape.

Thus did Elf and Dwarf share their knowledge with the descendants of their friends from long ago, those who had stood by them during long ages of ice and war. Then, with gifts given and friendships renewed, Elf and Dwarf went back into the wilderness or beneath the earth.

Dogging man every step of the way, however, were his ancient enemies, the forces of nature that would undo us: cold and fire, sea and storm. Many a Sea Giant gloated as he pulled a ship to the bottom of the deep, and many a Frost Giant buried a family under snow. And always, there was the Giant-nature inside us, the wrath and the coldness, the fire and the tempest, the reckless urges that must be mastered and made to serve.

Across the waves, too, came Blut and Boden. For the Elf-prince, it was a homecoming, a return after thousands of years to the land he loved. To Boden, you see, it was the soil that mattered most, the magic of this spot, this place, of being able to say, "Here is where my mother nursed me; here is where I grew up; here is where my father is buried." To remember by seeing, and to hand down a place made sacred by time to your children and grandchildren.

But for Blut, the Elf-princess, it was hard to leave Europe, and not just because it was her home. To her, it was always the bloodline that was foremost. For far longer than Boden, she had watched the sons of Arius grow into their elfish, dwarfish ways, and she loved them for it, like a mother adores her little children. She found delight in the magic of seeing the same face, the same trait, echo down through the generations, changed but a little, both old and new.

Of late, however, sorrow touched her heart at seeing so many sons of Arius depart for the sunset land. Then came the year the crops failed in Ireland, and one out of every four died of hunger. Almost as an entire people on the move, the Irish took to the sea.

Then Blut wept and said to her beloved, "Now is the time; I am ready. I must go with these troubled sons of Arius."

And so they crossed the ocean, Blut and Boden, and he showed her the lands and lakes where once stood the Elf kingdoms. For Boden, it was as yesterday, and he, too, wept. And together they lived in the great North Woods.

CHAPTER 6
A YOUNG BOY

And so my story moves to back where it began: near the Five Kingdoms, where a Giant youth once defied his own father and paid with his life, and his beloved shed ever-flowing tears for him. For thousands of years they lay there, bluffs facing bluffs across that beautiful, sad river that men call the Mississippi. Then the sons of Arius came and built towns along that river. And in the hills and ridges on either side, formed from those two Giants now turned to stone, they dug. With the skills that Dwarves had taught them long ago, men cut into the rock, broke it up, and with it made their homes.

One day, on one such spot, a group of men were laboring, and with them a boy named Hagen. He was an orphan, this boy, and hardly remembered his parents. His father had died in a great war fought between the sons of Arius in the North of this land and those in the South, a war between brothers. He remembered being very poor and hungry after that, and then his mother took sick and passed away. The loss of both parents would be hard for any child, and although Hagen was a clever boy and showed great promise, he let resentment at being an orphan get the better of him. Too often he used hardship as an excuse to be cruel. Although his mother's kin had taken him in, he ran away. Journeying far, he found work at a quarry where men cut into the rocky bluffs.

The quarry-men often had him go into small, tight places where they could not fit. When he was not needed for this, Hagen's task was to bring the men water and tools, since he was still too little to swing a hammer like they did. The work was hard, but now and then he had time to explore.

One chilly day in autumn, Hagen was off by himself, climbing stone that no hammer had yet struck. A cold wind whipped against him, and he was about to return to the worksite to warm himself by the fire when something caught his eye. Off to one side, on the bluff's surface, were letters etched into the stone unlike any Hagen had ever seen. Brush hid much of it, so he worked at removing the brambles. They scratched and pricked his hands, causing droplets of blood to fall upon the stone.

At last he could see the whole rockface, but he still had no idea what message it bore. Curiosity gripped him, but just then one of the men called out his name. Jealous that no one else should know of this discovery, he decided to return that night. The workmen would be asleep in the camp at the base of the bluffs, and he could examine the rock by the light of a torch.

Late that night, Hagen snuck out of the tent and made his way up to the worksite. The stars twinkled in a cloudless sky, and a half-moon lit his way, but he found it difficult to follow the path. Everything looked strange at night, and in the cold stillness, every noise made him pause, his heart pounding. Reaching the worksite at last, he found a torch and lit it with a flint-stone. With the fiery light to guide him, he retraced his steps up the bluff.

The rock here was steep, hard to scale even in the daytime, and several times he thought he would fall. Although the journey took only a few minutes, those minutes seemed like hours to Hagen. At last he reached the spot where he had seen the strange markings earlier.

By the light of the torch, Hagen could see the etchings, even stranger now in shadow and fire. Touching the stone, he ran his hand slowly down, tracing each letter, seeing the dark spots where his own blood had fallen earlier. Just when he had touched all of them, the ground rumbled, and the strange stone began to crack, breaking off in pieces. Dust rose, and he had to look away, coughing. When the rumbling stopped and the dust had settled, where once the carved stones had stood he saw an entrance, tall enough only for a child or short man. His heart was racing, but curiosity drove him on. Holding the torch before him, the boy stepped inside.

He found himself in a long tunnel, with smooth, round walls that arched just above his head. As he walked on, he noticed more strange letters along the walls. The tunnel sloped downward, then turned. This continued for a long while, until Hagen realized he must be following a spiral path down inside the rock.

After what seemed like an eternity, he emerged from the tunnel into a large cavern, with a dome that soared high above him. The walls here bore not only letters, but pictures, and he could tell that these told a story, or rather several stories. As the light from his torch flickered over the images, he shivered, even though it was less cold in here than outside.

One drawing showed a man casting one of his eyes into a pool of water. Elsewhere, three men walked toward two trees, and when they had left, the two trees had become a man and a woman. Another series of images depicted four men, one from each direction, coming together to work at a forge. When their task was finished, he saw that they had made a necklace, which they handed to a much taller woman with long hair.

When Hagen looked above at the top of the chamber, the light of his torch dimly revealed the image of a tree's branches. Lowering the torch, he saw that the branches entwined around every picture, as if they were all stories that had happened in one vast tree.

As he walked on, three stone chairs came into view along one side of the chamber. They looked to be thrones, and on each one sat a figure encased in armor, arms resting on an axe or sword. Helmets hid their faces and gauntlets covered their hands, but he had the distinct sense that the suits of armor were not empty. Whoever these figures had been, they were clearly shorter than most men, perhaps even his size. As he turned and brought his torch around, three other thrones appeared on the opposite side, and upon them three other armored figures.

It was dark ahead, for the chamber was longer than it was wide, and the light from his torch did not reach so far. But the desire to know overcame his fear, and he stepped forward. Out of the blackness a seventh throne appeared before him, larger than the others, and upon it another figure encased in metal. Its right hand rested upon a sword, its left upon a great hammer, both with ornate carvings that glinted in the torchlight. Standing before the throne, Hagen found himself at a loss. Who were these men, and how long had they been here?

Suddenly a voice spoke, not human, but as faint and rasping as the wind. The words came out slowly, as if with effort.

"Your face we have carved."

Hagen froze in terror. Surely he had imagined it? The thought of someone here with him chilled his blood. Again the voice spoke, this time less slowly and with more strength behind it.

"Your face, o son of Arius, how like the Elves it is. And yet it was the Giants who made it thus. In cold and snow, yes! But do not forget that the sun failed you so far north, and it was fire that kept you alive. Fire, the comfort of home and the bringer of ruin. But you can appreciate ruin, can you not, son of Arius?"

Hagen leaned forward a little, peering at the figure on the throne before him. Could this be the source of the voice? "Is it you?" he asked timidly.

This time the voice was angry: "I am not a tunnel-digging Dwarf! The seven sons of Mim lie dead here, though some say they do but sleep, waiting for the final battle. Well, I do not fear battle. And I do not lose my nerve, like the one who lies around us, Grim Jack's son."

"Wh-who are you?" Hagen sputtered.

"Can you not guess, boy? If I am here with you, but I am not the stones about you, or the Dwarf-lords within, what am I?"

Hagen had no idea.

"Then answer, Aryan boy, the riddle given by your ancestors:

"There is a warrior on earth, wondrously formed,
brightly made for men's use by two silent ones.
Foe against foe bears him in war, causing ruin,
yet despite his strength, women often bind him.
He obeys them well, serves them agreeably,
if men and maidens see to his needs.
If they govern him with care and feed him kindly,
he enriches their lives and brings joy.
But if they let him grow proud,
he repays them savagely.

"What am I?" the voice rasped.

Hagen thought about the words, but nothing came to mind. Then he noticed the torch in his hand.

"Are you... fire?"

A loud rush filled the chamber, and his torch flared up, tongues of flame reaching high above him.

"Yes, clever boy! But make no mistake – I am no servant!"

"Wh-what do you want?"

"The real question is what do *you* want? What reason has this world given you to want what it has to offer? It took your father, then it took your mother. Out in that cold night are warm houses where boys like yourself have mothers and fathers and are loved. Yet here I find you, all alone, loved by no one."

The words struck a chord deep within Hagen. Never had he felt so empty. And out of that emptiness grew hate, hatred for all those luckier than he.

The voice spoke. "We can destroy them, you and I. We can set the world on fire."

This idea gave him pause. As much as he hated, Hagen had not completely given in to the Giant-nature in him, not enough to stomach murder. If only he could have revenge some other way....

"Not destroy them," he replied, hoping his voice did not betray his fear. "Some other way."

The voice replied, "All right then, boy, we will not destroy. But let us be cleverer than they, at least. They have taken your past, so let us take theirs. Let us make them forget. They will sleepwalk through life."

"And what of me?" Hagen asked.

The voice seemed to smile. "You? You will be able to do what none of them can, trust me."

"How?"

"You need only perform a simple task. Look to the side of the throne, and you will find a basin."

Where the throne had cast a shadow before, Hagen's torch now revealed a small stand, resting on three legs. On it lay a broad-brimmed metal bowl. He stepped closer, and fire illuminated the inside of the basin, which he now saw held a liquid of sparkling gold. Beside it lay what looked like a bull's horn, but with strange letters carved upon it, and its tip and rim were covered in silver.

The fire spoke. "Fill the horn from the basin. Then walk down to the town by the river, to where men brew ale and the fires burn bright."

"I have seen it," Hagen said of the brewery.

"You will find a door on the river side that is always open. Enter it, and walk down the stairs to the cellar, where they have great open vats of ale. Do not speak to anyone. Wait until no one is looking, then walk up to a vat and empty the horn into it. Then leave at once, telling no one of what you've done."

"What is it?" Hagen asked of the liquid in the basin.

"Oh, my boy, that is the Ale of Forgetfulness! No one will be destroyed, you see. The sons of Arius will merely forget. They will be like men without a homeland, orphans of time."

Hagen felt himself capable of this task, yet still he hesitated. The mission was not without risk, if he should be caught. But oh, how he wanted power over his fellow men! And he didn't want it the other way, the way that is long and difficult. That path requires courage, and honor, and hard work. Hagen was impatient, eager to join a path that seems easy. But such a route never leads to manhood.

So he picked up the horn, lowered it into the basin, and filled it. Suddenly he heard a mournful, groaning sound – was it coming from the Dwarf-lords about him? He did not wait to find out. Horn in one hand, torch in the other, he left the cavern at once, never looking back as he rose through the long tunnel. His legs ached from the climb, but he did not stop until he was in the open air. Never was he so thankful as when he emerged from that place of doom.

Once outside, as he tried to catch his breath, Hagen noticed the torch in his hand and realized that he had never left the presence of the one who had spoken to him. Suddenly, the torch flared up in a dense cloud of sparks and was extinguished. Darkness engulfed Hagen. But the sparks, instead of flickering out in the black sky above the bluffs, only climbed higher, until a strong wind carried them off to the East.

It was a long journey from the bluff's height down to the plain and on into town, one that exhausted him. As he reached the first houses, dawn was already breaking over the top of the bluffs. People were busily setting about their daily tasks. Horses clip-clopped through the streets, pulling wagons loaded down with boxes or carriages filled with people. As he approached the brewery, crowds of workers were arriving. The stench here was strong, and it only got worse as he walked to the other side of the brewery, the river side.

Here where men burned trash, he saw the flames burning bright against the still-dark western sky. To Hagen, their flickering seemed like a language whose sounds were familiar but whose words were foreign. Rough-looking men, hitching up mules to carts filled with barrels, were too busy to notice a boy slipping inside an open door.

Holding his nose to block the stench, Hagen descended the stairs to the depths below. Here more workers moved about, but if any saw Hagen, they thought him another boy hired to crawl into small spaces to fix their machines. No one noticed that this boy clutched an odd horn to his body.

Hagen kept off to one side until the men were all busy peering around one vat. With his heart threatening to burst, he approached another vat and poured the horn's contents inside. He turned at once and walked away, but his walk soon became a run, for he did not care now if anyone saw him, just so long as he could get out of there.

Rushing up the stairs, he ran straight into a bearded man no taller than himself. When the man saw the horn clutched in Hagen's hands, he gripped him about the shoulders. His gray eyes looked like cut stone and had a fierce glint about them.

"What have you done, boy?" he demanded. "What have you done?"

Hagen panicked, dropping the horn. When the man leapt for it, Hagen bolted past him, climbing as fast as his legs could carry him. Once up the stairs and through the door, he turned to see if the man had followed him. He hadn't.

Leaning against the wall, gasping for breath, Hagen watched the fires, which now seemed to reach even higher into the sky. The area was now deserted, the men gone. In a nearby tree, two birds perched, twittering and chirping to each other. They fascinated him, as if the events of last night and this morning had never happened, and he were a mere boy at play.

He became aware of a throbbing pain in one thumb. From the look of it, he must have cut himself on the horn's silver edges when he gripped it. Instinctively, he put his cut thumb into his mouth. In that moment, Hagen heard the birds again, only now he understood their speech.

"Poor boy," chirped one. "He doesn't know what he has done."

"Little does he suspect the Giant," piped the other one. "Shouldn't have trusted him."

Hagen listened, enthralled. Another bird landed on a nearby branch, a dark raven. Its cawing, too, came to him with the clarity of human speech:

"Fire in the East! Fire in the East! Five fires for the sons of Arius!"

Before he could ponder the meaning of these words, Hagen began to feel very strange. He had a sudden thirst for water, not just to drink it but to dive into it. The desire grew stronger, and he found himself heading toward the river, desperately breaking into a run. His hands and feet began to throb, and he found it hard to breathe, but still he ran, for the need to enter the water was overpowering.

When he reached the dock where the steamboats landed, he

sped down the planks. Dimly aware that people around were shouting at him, his only thought was to reach the water. Barely breathing, with one last supreme effort Hagen leapt off the edge of the dock.

As his body entered the water, it was transformed, inch by inch, into a fish. Newly formed gills greedily took in the water now so needed for breathing. His clothes slid off his slick fish-body and floated away, to the great worry of those nearby, who saw only that a boy entered the water and did not come up.

But Hagen was still alive, deep below the surface. Only now, as a fish, his memory was worse than any man's. He did not remember who he was, or how he got there, or whether things had ever been any different than they now were.

Do you want to be like that, dear reader? To not know who you are, or how you got here, or whether the world has ever been any different from the way it is now? But I tell you, there are millions all around you who walk about in that state of mind. So let us leave this fish, who was once a boy named Hagen, for he will be in the river a long time – in fact, you may still catch sight of him. He will look like any fish, I suppose, only there will be something a bit human about his eyes. And as the Giant slyly promised, he can now do what no man can.

CHAPTER 7
NIGHT OF FIRE

Let us now go to where the brewery's waste-water empties into the river. Watch as it reaches that river of tears that Gerda sheds for her beloved. See the bubbles floating right there, the ones just now flowing into the river? That is the Ale of Forgetfulness, entering the mightiest river of this sunset land. As each river and stream flows into it, that magical ale follows them up to their sources and back down again, rushing on toward the ocean. And far away in the sunrise land of Europe surges another great river, the Rhine, flowing through the lake where Boden once felled the Winter King. There another boy – perhaps also named Hagen – has unleashed forgetfulness for the sons of Arius who dwell there.

But we must return now to Hagen's river, and go forward as if time itself were a stream. Moving along, we see men building a bridge to cross the span, and the first train crossing Gerda's tearful stream. Floating down the river of time, we start to see trucks and cars, and then high above, airplanes, whose passengers scarcely notice the tiny blue line far below. Wondrous inventions, these, many times faster than a horse, stronger than a hundred oxen, and soaring higher than eagles. Machines that come from the creative minds and hard work of the sons of Arius, still benefiting from their Elf-nature and Dwarf-nature.

But something else is coming to pass. This race is becoming more forgetful – not all at once like Hagen, but gradually, each generation more than the one before. This town, like so many others, bustles with sons of Arius from the old lands of Europe. Yet they are forgetting the speech of their parents and grandparents, forgetting also their traditions, forgetting their virtues even. If they continue to forget, soon I fear they will be like the Hagen-fish that still haunts the river's depths.

Watch them now, as once more they set off across the ocean, returning to their ancestral lands only to fight their brethren in a terrible war. See those two men in the trenches, dead but clutched in an embrace? They bear the same last name, cousins who died by each other's hand.

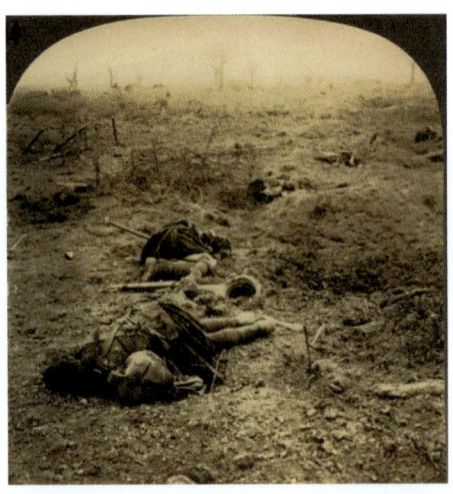

Now watch, only a generation later, as their children cross the ocean again, and the race of Arius tears itself apart in another war. By the millions they fall, with little glory, in a brothers' war, forgetting that their ancestors were forged in the same frost-bitten land. And the more they forget, the less they have to pass on.

Let us return to that scene of Hagen by the river. Do you see that young girl on the dock, trying to find the body of the poor boy who just jumped in? She has nine sisters and brothers. One of ten herself, she will grow up to have six children, and they in turn will have only four. Perhaps, as she tells the story of that day to her grandchildren, she will notice that there are fewer about than when her grandfather told stories of the old country, speaking the old tongue. They do not speak it, these grandchildren of hers; they do not even understand it. But they are so much smarter, with so many new *things*.

When these grandchildren grow up, most will have only two children, and those, in turn, will have but one child, or perhaps none at all. That generation will not even know what language it was that their great-great-grandfather spoke, or what things their great-great-grandmother could do. They will have no idea of how they loved, the stories they cherished, the lands they left, or the hardships they overcame. But they will be ever so much smarter than people were in the old days! The proof is right here, in the devices they hold in their hands – see, forgetfulness is no problem! But truly, you can forget only what you have first known, and soon they will know so little, even the forgetting will be at an end.

See how men and women forget even their own nature. The sharp contrast between manliness and feminine grace fades away, leaving confusion and unhappiness. Over time, they draw away from the fine elfin form and noble features of their ancestors. Fading, too, is the dwarfish toughness inside by which their forefathers tamed continents. The sons of Arius grow weak, timid, and cheerless.

Listen as they teach their children to be ashamed of their ancestors, to take no pride in their bright-shining race. Little wonder, then, that when these children grow up, so many throw away the legacy of thousands of years and mix their blood with other races. The uniqueness of Blut's Gift means nothing to them. Soon they will bear no resemblance at all to the radiant Mistress of the Elves. They will all be brown in skin, brown in hair, brown in eyes, and it will be as if the sons of Arius never were.

They betray not only their blood, but the soil their ancestors fought so hard to win. This land, which generations of men and women and children paid for with sweat and blood, produces more wealth than ever thanks to that sacrifice. Now watch as their descendants simply give it away, opening the floodgates to all the races of the world. So much forgetting, where will it end?

But let us now return to the bluffs on that autumn night. As Hagen scrambles down on his grim mission, we follow the path of those sparks that the wind carried off to the East. One spark flies toward the southern edge of the lake where Boden's kingdom once stood. Here the sons of Arius have built a great city, Chicago. The tiny spark drops down into a barn, where it begins to feed on hay and wood. Tiny at first, the flame quickly grows into a blaze that lights up the night sky. It spreads to the lumber yards, and to the ships along the lake. A cold wind blows in from the West and spreads it far and wide. The mightiest city on the five lakes is afire, and a hundred thousand people flee!

Another spark leaves the bluff and heads east, but farther north upon the lakeshore. This will become the deadliest fire of them all, a firestorm blazing its way across the land. Farmers flee the inferno only to find every way blocked by the flames. Watch as three more sparks from Hagen's torch travel across the Great Lakes, starting

The Great Fires of Oct. 8, 1871

Peshtigo • Manistee • Huron • Holland • Chicago

vast fires that burn on into the day, and into the following night.

The fires bring tragedy, but the struggle calls forth great acts of heroism. In the deep forests, where settlers strive to contain the blaze, here and there you can see a stout, bearded stranger arrive to help. Watch as his axe, gleaming in the firelight, cuts down tree after tree to prevent the fire's spread. He leads the men in digging a ditch to keep the flames from reaching a settlement. Never did you see such strength and perseverance!

Over there, look at that family huddled outside their cabin, fire all around them, with nowhere to go. The flicker of flames on shadowy faces shows a curious scene, for here it is not the children who weep, but the parents, for they are wise enough to know their doom. But what is this? Their youngest daughter sees someone walking through the flames, but her parents do not believe her. The girl runs toward the fire, while her mother and father cry out, chasing after her, even though death is certain anyway.

But who is that emerging from the blaze? All three stop in their tracks, struck dumb. A woman steps out from the sheet of fire, and she seems untroubled and oh! how beautiful. The light dances on copper-red hair and eyes of amber flecked with gold. On her chest lies a pendant shaped like a heart, seeming to whirl within more than the flames without. Stepping out of the flames, she beckons to them.

The parents gather their little ones, then watch as she walks toward the fiery wall, calm and confident. How that fire wants her! To take the Mistress of the Elves, and the Radiant Heart upon her breast as well! The blaze surges all around, but she merely raises her hand and it falls back. As they follow her, a tunnel in the fire opens up, and on either side the flames subside, as if kneeling before her. The fire yields not willingly, but grudgingly, fighting it every moment yet powerless to resist.

On they walk, until by the light of day they reach safety. When the parents turn to thank her, they see a woman not with auburn hair, but blond, yet with the same enchanting face. They cannot know that in their faces, and those of their children, she recognizes other faces, of which these are the distant echoes. She sees the faces of those who stood by her through ages of ice, the men who charged with Boden in the Winter War, as well as the women who welcomed them home, and the children they bore.

Not far from this scene, Boden stands at the edge of the lake that lies between these fires. With his sharp Elf eyes he can see the blazes burning on the far shores, to the East and far to the South, where Chicago now lies in ruins. If we listen very closely, we can make out a rasping, inhuman voice coming from the flames nearby:

"Elf-prince, behold what was once your kingdom, destroyed now a second time. Half lies drowned beneath the water; the half above lies in flames. See how the sons of Arius flee in terror, just like your brethren did when Grim Jack placed his icy boot on the Five Kingdoms. What he could not finish, I now do."

The voice went on, seeming to grin. "Where you see a goodly frame, this middle-earth, I will make a barren land. Where you see a most excellent canopy, the wondrous overhanging sky, a majestical roof, I will consume with golden fire, until nothing is left but a foul and pestilent throng of vapors."

Boden did not turn around but kept his eyes on the distant fires across the water. "I know you, Wildfire, for always you were the most hateful of the Fire Giants. Your hatred for Elves I know, but the sons of Arius – why do you despise them?"

"Ah, prince, how like an Elf are the sons of Arius! How noble their mind, how infinite their inventiveness, in appearance how admirable! In action how like a Dwarf, as they struggle to tame this land and make a future for their children. The beauty of the world, a race to envy! And yet to me, what is this Elf-like, Dwarf-like race but a pile of dust, waiting to be blown away?

"They live but a day, yet they pay no heed to what came before them, or what may come after. On a whim they waste their inheritance, changing so much from one moment to the next that they destroy the fabric of their own society. The chain is broken; one generation cannot link with another. And after each man's brief day, it is as if he had never been. The sons of Arius, you say? Better to call them the flies of summer."

"It is not so," Boden replied, "for they remember more than you say they do, and they pass it down. The line is not broken, and in that continuance lies an eternity that even an Elf might envy. Yet they do have some of the Giant in them, that I will admit. Between the hot fires of rage and lust and the cold frosts of indifference and apathy, they do abandon their better selves."

At this, Wildfire roared in anger: "Better self, you call it? Or do they but return to their true nature? My cousin the West Wind now fans the flames higher, and soon Sister Drought and Brother Famine will arrive. And this winter, the Frost Giants will bring great misery to men. Then we will see how noble they are!

"But nothing compares to what I have done this night in the place where the Dwarf-lords slumber. Now the last links in the chain of memory will snap, and the sons of Arius will utterly abandon the ways of their ancestors. You will soon shudder to think of any resemblance with them."

Boden's alarm could be heard in his voice. "You speak of the Ale of Forgetfulness?" He turned to face the flames behind him.

"Yes!" the voice hissed eagerly. "Even now, they draw it in their water to fight the fire in vain, and they drink it from ladles held out to them. It flows even in the sea that bears your name. Across the continents, the sons of Arius begin their long fall from the heights. But first I will burn and raze the land of the Five Kingdoms, ridding it of Elves, Dwarves, and men alike."

Boden, crestfallen, knew that he could not undo the ale's magic. Yet as he looked at the flames all about, he realized that it was his duty to defend the Five Kingdoms. It was a birthright he had never claimed, for those kingdoms had fallen ages ago, before he first set out across the ocean. But did those realms not live on? Not just in the great North Woods, and in the few Elf-bands and Dwarf-troops that lived there, but in the sons of Arius?

They were still a young race. Like a wayward child, they often fell into error, but they showed great promise. No other race carried Blut's Gift. No other race created endlessly, impatient to reach other worlds. No other race was carved by glaciers, inside and out, into something an Elf might admire. The world would be much poorer without them. No, he could not allow them to perish in this fiery holocaust. But how to stop it?

He walked toward the shore. Once, many thousands of years ago, a magnificent hall stood not far from here, in a place now engulfed by water. Somewhere, far below the surface that now shimmered by the light of the flames, sat his father, and upon his hand, the ring of kingship. It was time for Boden to claim his inheritance.

The Elf-prince walked into the water, while Wildfire crackled triumphantly. When the water had reached his chest, Boden dove down, following the sloping shelf toward the bottom of the lake called Michigan. Elves can swim far more swiftly, and their bodies preserve the breath far longer, than any man. Deep beneath the surface, in a place known only to him, the Elf-prince entered a tunnel. With great speed he followed it into a great cavern, the place of his father's royal court.

There, at the end of that once-glorious hall, stood two thrones, and upon them an Elf-king and his queen. Through long ages, their bodies had been preserved without blemish, for nature has no power to decay the bodies of Elves or age them in any way. Boden looked upon his father, who bore the death-wound from Grim Jack's spear, an event that now seemed as but yesterday to the prince. Beside the monarch sat his queen, Boden's mother, who had died from a broken heart for the loss of her darling husband and the fall of their realm. Her hand had been placed in his by attentive servants, while their sky-blue eyes looked straight ahead, forever watching over their kingdom beneath the sea.

Boden approached this scene not with dread but with a longing and sadness such as only the long-lived Elves can know. He swam to his father's side, and in his ear mouthed these words: "Father, I have returned." As his father's eyes continued to stare forward, Boden slipped the ancient ring from his hand. Turning to his mother, he lovingly kissed the cheek of the one who had cried so much for him. Then he left the watery hall where once he had played as a child.

When Boden returned to the surface, the fires were still raging fiercely. Near the shore, the Fire Giant laughed his dry laugh at seeing him emerge from the lake.

"What is this? I thought you had left to save yourself, the way your father once failed to do!"

"No," Boden said, his voice steely. "It is him I went to seek."

"The lake will never give up her dead, Elf-prince. But have no worry, you will soon join them in death."

"You speak to no prince, Wildfire, but a king!" Boden declared in a commanding voice.

"You have no kingdom left!" the fire rasped. "And no subjects."

"There you are mistaken. My kingdom is this land, and subjects enough I have: the Elves who have returned, the deep-digging Dwarves, and the true-born sons of Arius. For despite the Ale of Forgetfulness, some of Arius' race will remember. They will grow strong in Elf-nature and Dwarf-nature, and I will fight for them."

At this the Fire Giant scoffed. "You may fight for them, Elf, but I tell you, they will not even fight for themselves. In years to come, the sons of Arius will not even lift a finger to save what is theirs, and when their enemies cast them to the ground, they will apologize for being in the way. The world will rejoice to be rid of such a craven race. Do you doubt it? Fair enough. I will see that you live to etch their memory on a gravestone, and long enough to see those etchings fade from sight."

"The fewer the true sons of Arius that remain," Boden replied, "the harder they will fight. Such has always been the Aryan way."

Then that lord of Elves raised his hand, and on it was his father's royal ring, shining with blue-green gems expertly placed there by Dwarf-smiths long ago. A rumble shook heaven and earth, and dark clouds gathered overhead.

"What is this?" rasped the fire.

"Bow before your king, Wildfire." And with that a thunderclap ripped across the sky, and rain began to fall. It quickly grew to a torrent, and not just there at the water's edge, but throughout Boden's realm. All around the lakes, the fires let loose upon the landscape began to die down, struggling to devour in vain. Wildfire raged, but the sound grew harder to hear as the rain beat down upon him. The flames lowered reluctantly to the ground, sputtered, then were no more.

Then the wind became still, and all that could be heard was the rainfall, renewing the land, giving hope to the people. In burnt-out farms and cities across Boden's realm, the sons of Arius thanked the strangers who had helped them, and those strangers went back into the wilderness. As the rain finally came to an end, the sun emerged once more, and the sons of Arius set about the work to be done.

They rebuilt.

And somewhere Gerda continued to shed her tears, and men crossed her river without knowing it. Somewhere a strange fish moved in the waters, and when he surfaced, glimpsed tongues of fire burning in the distance, and he tried to remember but could not. Somewhere deep inside a rocky bluff lay a cave with seven Dwarf-lords inside, silently awaiting the final battle. Somewhere beneath a lake stood another cave, where a king and queen of Elves sat in their watery hall. And somewhere, deep in the forest, the most valiant of Elves turned to her of the Radiant Heart, and said, "Come, my queen." And they walked off, hand in hand.

And somewhere people are asleep even though they walk about. Yet somewhere, too, children dream of things truer than what they know when awake. And somewhere visions still stir the blood and take firm root in the soil.

EVERY END IS A BEGINNING

HISTORICAL NOTE

The fires depicted in this book did occur. On October 8, 1871, five major fires occurred across the Great Lakes region, affecting the states of Michigan, Wisconsin, and Illinois. The fire in Wisconsin is called the Peshtigo Fire and remains the deadliest wildfire in American history. It created what is called a firestorm, in which the fire creates its own wind system. The fire in Illinois is called the Great Chicago Fire. Altogether, around 2,000 people lost their lives in these five fires.

To this day, why five great fires should occur on the same night, separated by such great distances, remains unexplained. In more recent years, some have argued that the cause may have come from space: perhaps fragments from a comet fell to earth and started the fires in all these places. Others disagree, arguing that meteorites are not burning when they hit the earth. A rock large enough to generate that kind of heat on impact would leave a massive crater, yet no crater, much less five, has been found.

In any event, an unexpected rainfall toward the evening of October 9th helped bring an end to the fires.

CREDITS

Front Cover: Andrew Lang, *Tales of the Round Table*, illustration by H.J. Ford, *Lancelot Bears Off Guenevere*. Public domain.

2 Joseph Wright of Derby, *Vesuvius From Portici*. Public domain.
3 Image 1: Johan Christian Dahl, *Megalith Grave in Winter*. Public domain. Image 2: Albert Bierstadt, *Storm in the Mountains*. Public domain.
4 Thomas Moran, *Sunset Near Land's End, Cornwall*. Public domain.
5 Edward Robert Hughes R.W.S., *Midsummer Eve*. Public domain.
7 Akseli Gallen-Kallela, *The Forging of the Sampo*. Public domain.
10 John Charles Dollman, *The Giant with the Flaming Sword*. Public domain.
11 Map of North American glaciation by Thomas C. Chamberlin. Courtesy of Wikimedia Commons. Public domain.
12 William Charles Piguenit, *Hawkesbury River with Figures in Boat: On the Nepean*. Image has been slightly modified. Public domain.
13 Map of the Great Lakes basin by Wikimedia user Drdpw. (CC BY-SA 3.0)
15 Detail from Edmund Blair Leighton, *In Time of Peril*. Public domain.
18 Johannes Gehrts, *Freyr*. Public domain.
19 Map of Europe during the last glacial period. Courtesy of Wikimedia Commons user Ulamm. Modified from original to include place-names. (CC BY-SA 3.0)
20 Photo of Finsteraarhorn by Wikimedia user Tom Bärfuss. Public domain.
23 Arthur Hughes, *Ophelia ("And He Will Not Come Back Again")*. Public domain.
25 John William Waterhouse, *La Belle Dame Sans Merci*. Public domain.
29 Edmund Blair Leighton, *The Accolade*. Public domain.
30 Edwin Landseer, *The Monarch of the Glen*. Public domain.
32 Viktor Vasnetsov, *After Prince Igor's Battle with the Polovtsi*. Public domain.
33 Map of Lake Constance ("Bodensee" in German). Public domain.
35 Photo of Senja Island, Norway. Courtesy of Wikimedia Commons user Ximonic/Simo Räsänen (CC BY-SA 4.0).
36 Photo of Rakotzbrücke, Germany. Courtesy of Wikimedia Commons user A. Landgraf (CC BY-SA 4.0).
38 Albert Bierstadt, *Sierra Nevada*. Public domain.

39	Emanuel Leutze, *Westward the Course of Empire Takes Its Way*. Public domain.
41	Photo of prospecting for gold, 1858. Public domain.
43	John William Waterhouse, *The Tempest*. Public domain.
46	Photo of Grandad Bluff with a quarry operation in the foreground. Courtesy of Wikimedia Commons. Public domain.
47	Photo of runestone in Glavendruplunden, Funen, Denmark. Courtesy of Wikimedia Commons user Danielle Keller(CC BY-SA 3.0). Image has been cropped and turned sideways.
58	Photo of Altes Eisinger Loch near Neulingen, Germany. Courtesy of Wikimedia user Hans-Peter Scholz (CC BY-SA 3.0). Image has been cropped and rendered in black and white.
51	Photo of torch courtesy of Wikimedia Commons user Pxhere (CC0).
53	Postcard of the G. Heileman Brewing Company. Image courtesy of the Wisconsin Historical Society. Public domain.
55	Robert W. Hines, *Arctic Grayling (Thymallus arcticus) leaping for a fly fisherman's bait*. Courtesy of Wikimedia Commons. Public domain.
58	Photo, "Proud Men of the North Who Fought on Flanders Fields." Courtesy of Wikimedia Commons. Public domain.
60	Illustration of Chicago in Flames, Currier & Ives. Courtesy of Wikimedia Commons. Public domain.
61	Image 1: Map of 1871 fire created by author using public domain imagery of the Great Lakes from Wikimedia Commons. Image 2: Illustration of the Peshtigo Fire, Harper's Weekly. Courtesy of the Wisconsin Historical Society. Public domain.
62	Harry George Theaker, *Sigyn Loki's Wife*, from *Children's Stories from the Northern Lands*. Public domain.
63	Illustration of the Burning of the Chicago River, Currier & Ives. Courtesy of Wikimedia Commons. Public domain.
64	Photo of the Chicago Fire, 1871, courtesy of Wikimedia Commons. Public domain.
68	Viktor Vasnetsov, *Knight at the Crossroads*. Public domain.
69	John William Waterhouse, *Isolde with the Potion*. Public domain.

Note 1: Wildfire's riddle is Riddle 8 from *Anglo-Saxon Riddles of the Exeter Book*. Original text accessed through Wikisource, translation by the author.
Note 2: Information in Historical Note is taken from the Wikipedia articles on the Peshtigo Fire and the Great Chicago Fire.

Printed in Poland
by Amazon Fulfillment
Poland Sp. z o.o., Wrocław